Wizzie Witch

Colin & Jacqui Hawkins

PictureLions

An Imprint of HarperCollinsPublishers

First published in Great Britain in Picture Lions by HarperCollins Publishers in 1999

1 3 5 7 9 10 8 6 4 2

ISBN: 0 00 664702 2

Picture Lions is an imprint of the Children's Division,
part of HarperCollins Publishers Ltd.
Text copyright © Colin and Jacqui Hawkins 1999
Illustrations copyright © Colin and Jacqui Hawkins 1999, 1981
The authors assert the moral right to be identified as the authors of the work.
A CIP catalogue record for this title is available from the British Library.
The HarperCollins website address is: www.fireandwater.com
Printed and bound in Singapore by Imago

Which Witch?

If you could be a witch,

which witch would you be?

Would you be a batty

witch, with lots of bats?

Or would you be a catty

witch, with lots of cats?

All witches are scatty,

with tall, pointy hats.

Wizzie Witch

Meet Wizzie Witch and her pet crow, Mo.

"I'm a whizz at magic," chuckles Wizzie.

Wizzie is a charming old witch who collects vegetables and weeds for her spells. Like all witches she has to practise her magic every day or spells can go wrong, like the time she turned the postman into a toad by mistake.

Witch House

Wizzie Witch lives in a very old, dark, creaky house called Cauldron Cottage at 13, Spooky Lane, Witchwood. Wizzie's cottage is cosy, creepy, warm and snug and has been her home for many, many years. There are cobweb curtains at the windows, bats in the attic, cats in every corner and spiders in every nook.

"My old cottage has everything a witch could wish for; even a broomshed for my broomstick," chuckles Wizzie.

Witch Magic

A witchy way to start the day
is to make a spell.
"It's magic, making magic," says
Wizzie, as she opens up her
Big Bumper Book of Spells and Secrets.
Today Wizzie makes a spell to
cure smelly feet. Into her black pot she pops 3 spiders'
webs, a bucket of rainwater, Double Bubble bubblegum,
mashed nettles and one teaspoonful of snail trail slime.
As the magic mix gurgles and burbles, Wizzie stirs it well
for ten minutes and chants —

"Spider webs and stings,
Are the very things,
To cure a foot smell,
This spell works well.
Just rub on the lotion,
Of this magic potion."

Witch Spells

Wizzie is a whizz at making spells.
Here are some of her favourites!

Bus Spell

Chant ten times:
Bus, bus don't be late,
I really, really cannot wait!

Toothache Spell

Put sleepy mole around neck and whisper:
Sleepy Mole, please I beg,
Take this pain from my toothy peg.

Rainmaking Spell

Repeat ten times:

Pitter, patter, splitter, splatter,
Pitter, splatter, splitter, patter.

Toad into a Prince Spell

Kiss toad three times and hiss:

Toady, Toady, kiss, kiss, kiss!

Cut Finger Spell

Sprinkle salt on sleeping dog and shout:

Salt on mutt, cure this cut.

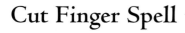

Witch

Every morning when Wizzie gets
dressed, she puts on her vest and
thick red knickers. Then she pulls
on long, thick black stockings,
buttons up her bodywarmer and
pulls on her fingerless gloves.
Wizzie always wears warm clothes,
especially when she is flying on
her broomstick.

"I think it's best, to wear
a vest!" she giggles.

Wear

Like all witches, Wizzie's favourite colour is black.

"It doesn't show the dirt," she cackles.

She puts on a long, black dress with lots of secret pockets for keeping witchy things like toads, spell-books, chewing gum, slugs and snails.

Wizzie laces up her boots and straightens her pointy witch's hat.

"Now I look enchanting!" laughs Wizzie as she flies off.

Witch Pets

Wizzie shares Cauldron Cottage with lots of witchy pets. They gather up all the secrets and news of Witchwood and whisper them to Wizzie.

"They're all very familiar," she cackles. There's Mo the crow, Scoot the spider, Twit the wise old owl, Snap the baby crocodile, and Hocus the cat, who helps to make Wizzie's spells purr-fect. Hubble and Bubble the bats just hang around, and Wart the toad lives in the magic kettle.

Witch Weed

Every day, Wizzie spends a bewitching hour in her garden. She grows lots of plants and vegetables for her magic spells and potions. Wizzie's garden is full of potty potatoes, mushy mushrooms, leaky leeks and pushy peas.

She has stingy nettles, snappy snapdragons, spotty toadstools, brambly briars and thorny thistles. Wizzie has every witch weed a green-fingered witch could wish for.

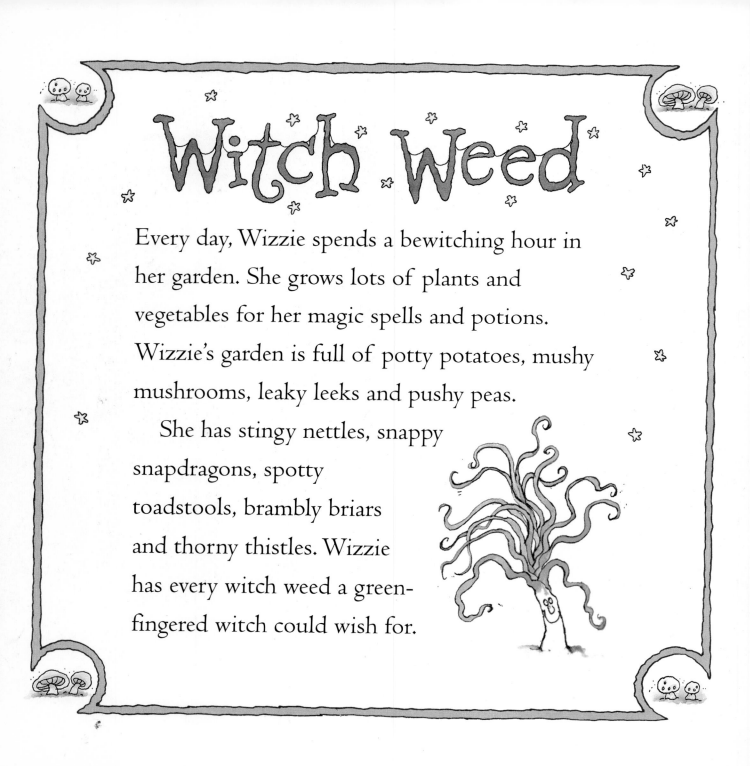

Witch Shops

"Let's go shopping," says Wizzie to
Hocus the cat as they peer into the
empty pantry. So Wizzie goes to the butcher, the baker,
the candlestick maker and then
flies off to *Trick or Treats*, her
local supermarket.

"I need weed
feed, bird seed, carrot stew, stuff for
the loo, sugar and spice, a big choc
ice, lots of grubs and worms in
tubs," chants Wizzie.

not a witch

Then Wizzie meets her witchy friend Wilma and they
have great fun trolley-racing round the supermarket.

"Last one to the checkout is a silly snail," she cackles.

Witch Food

Wizzie gives her friends Wendy, Wanda and Wilma a magic tea party.

She serves icky-sticky buns, magic muffins, wicked chocolate cake, wibbly-wobbly jelly and lots of weedy tea.

"What does the future hold for you?" says Wizzie, as she peers into Wilma's teacup and reads her tea leaves. "You're going to meet a tall, dark stranger."

"Wizard!" laughs Wilma.

Witch Wash

At the end of another spellbinding day, Wizzie enjoys a hot hubble-bubble bath. She loves to soak in the big tin tub, as Hocus the cat gives her back a scrub, and the magic kettle brings more hot water.

To make herself even more enchanting, Wizzie uses lots of lotions and potions in her bath like Mumbo-Jumbo Bath Gel, Abracadabra Bath Salts, Spelly Smelly Soap, Stinky-Poo Shampoo and Witch Wash 'n' Go.

"A clean witch is a happy witch," bubbles Wizzie.

Witch Dreams

As it gets dark Wizzie lights the candles. The shadows lengthen and dark corners creep nearer. "It's time for bed. I need my beauty sleep," she yawns.

Wizzie climbs into her bed and snuggles into the cobwebby blankets.

It's not long before she falls fast asleep and dreams witchy dreams.

Goodnight WizzZZzie!